THE FUNNY LITTLE BOY

By Dorothy Walter Baruch

Pictures by Lietta

LOTHROP, LEE and SHEPARD COMPANY

Boston New York

1936

LITHOGRAPHED IN THE UNITED STATES OF AMERICA
BY DUENEWALD PRINTING CORPORATION

THE FUNNY LITTLE BOY

ONCE there was a little boy. They called him Sneeger. He went through the day with skipping feet. He liked funny things. He liked to laugh. There were so many things in the world to laugh at.

A little girl moved into the house next door. They called her Lorna. Sneeger saw that her feet were slow and that she had a frown between her eyes. The corners of her mouth turned down. She never sang. She never laughed.

"Poor Lorna," thought Sneeger. He wanted her to play with him, but all she would do was stand with the frown between her eyes and stare sadly.

And then one day, Sneeger had an idea. He would show Lorna something funny. He would make her laugh and if she once laughed with him she would play with him. It would be easy.

"Look Lorna," he cried, "I'll show you something funny."

With that he took off his shoes. And he took off his socks. And he took off his sweater. Then he put his legs through the arms of his sweater as if the arms were trousers. And he put a sock on each of his EARS. And he put a shoe on each of his hands and wiggled them.

But Lorna did not laugh. She did not even smile. She just frowned and looked sad and ever so gloomy.

So Sneeger took his red bucket from the sand box. Up, he put it, on top of his head. And then quickly he bent his head forward so that the bucket dropped, plop-bong kerplop, down, onto the ground.

But Lorna did not laugh. She only looked sad and ever so gloomy.

Sneeger must try something else. He climbed onto his swing. But instead of making the swing go straight back and forth, he made it jiggle and go crooked—wobbeldy wobbeldy from side to side.

It felt funny. Maybe it would make Lorna laugh. But no, it didn't.

So Sneeger took his teddy bear. He climbed with it to the top of his high slide. There he gave it a push.

Swish, the teddy bear went lickety down the slide and turned a sprawling somersault at the bottom.

But Lorna did not laugh. She still looked sad and ever so gloomy.

"Oh dear," sighed Sneeger, "I wish I could make her laugh. But it isn't so easy!"

So he sat down and thought and thought.

And as he was sitting, he spied the old lady who lived behind his house carrying a waste-basket full of papers to burn when all of a sudden a wind started blowing. And puff, the papers from the basket blew UP into the air. Some blew this way. Some blew that way. This way! That way! Puff! Everywhere the papers flew.

It looked so funny, Sneeger had to laugh. "Look," he cried to Lorna.

But not a laugh did she laugh, not a smile did she smile. She kept right on looking sad and ever so gloomy.

Sneeger must try again.

So he picked a brown stick from among the flowers where it lay. He carried it to a big tub of water that stood in the laundry yard, and with the stick he *slapped* the water—so that the water splattered, splash, splash, SPLASH!

And he stirred the water and stirred and sang,

"Mungaloo, mungaloo
Mud, mud
Mud pudding!"

He had to laugh. Surely Lorna would too. But no, she still looked sad and ever so gloomy.

And then Sneeger had several ideas all at one time.

"I can kick like a horse," said Sneeger; and he kicked his legs out friskily behind him.

"I can sit up and bark like a dog," said Sneeger. And he sat on his haunches and barked "Gruff wuff, bow-wow wow wow!" And he hung his tongue out the way dogs do.

"And I can hop like a rabbit. . . ."

"And make my mouth go like a gold-fish. . . ."

Still Lorna did not laugh, but went right on looking sad and ever so gloomy.

Then Sneeger ran onto the lawn. And there he jumped and went FLOP and rolled over and kicked and kicked his feet. And he laughed because it seemed so funny.

But Lorna just stared sadly at him.

It was then that Sneeger felt something tickling his face. With his finger he found that it was a lady-bug crawling up his nose—creeping, crawling—slowly up his nose. He let it crawl on slowly, while he laughed again.

"See?" he asked Lorna.

But never a smile did Lorna smile. Her face was still sad and ever so gloomy.

Sneeger stood still. He didn't know what else to do. He had tried so many things. But nothing had done any good.

"Dear, oh dear, oh dear," sighed Sneeger.

He didn't feel like laughing any more himself. He felt sad and he looked sad. Sneeger looked SAD and ever so GLOOMY. His feet felt slow, the corners of his mouth turned down, and a frown had come between his eyes. He stared sadly at Lorna.

And then—all of a sudden—

Lorna opened her mouth and *started to laugh.* She laughed and laughed. Sneeger couldn't understand it. He didn't see anything funny just then to laugh at.

"Oh look, oh look," laughed Lorna. And she pointed at Sneeger. "Sneeger, you're so funny when you look that sad and gloomy. I never thought you could look so funny!"

Then Sneeger knew why Lorna was laughing. And he started to laugh too, and together they laughed and laughed.

Now Lorna would play with him. She was no longer sad and ever so gloomy. Sneeger at last had made her laugh.